TEENY WITCH

Goes to the LIBRARY

by LIZ MATTHEWS
illustrated by CAROLYN LOH

D1551007

Troll Associates

Library of Congress Cataloging-in-Publication Data

Matthews, Liz.
    Teeny Witch goes to the library / by Liz Matthews; illustrated by
Carolyn Loh.
       p.   cm.
    Summary: On a rainy day Teeny Witch visits the library, where she
sees a pet exhibit, enjoys a puppet show, and reads an exciting
horse story.
    ISBN 0-8167-2268-4 (lib. bdg.)   ISBN 0-8167-2269-2 (pbk.)
    [1. Libraries—Fiction. 2. Witches—Fiction.] I. Loh, Carolyn,
ill. II. Title.
PZ7.M4337Tj 1991
[E]—dc20   90-11140

Copyright © 1991 by Troll Associates
All rights reserved. No portion of this book may be reproduced in any
form, electronic or mechanical, including photocopying, recording, or
information storage and retrieval systems, without prior written
permission from the publisher. Printed in the U.S.A.
10   9   8   7   6   5   4   3   2

Pitter! Patter! Splatter!
Teeny Witch felt awful. She couldn't find anything fun to do. She sat by a wide window and watched the rain.

Teeny got up. She went into the kitchen where Aunt Icky was making cookies.

"What is wrong?" Aunt Icky asked Teeny. "You look so sad."

"I am bored," groaned Teeny Witch. "I have nothing to do."

"You could play with toys in your room," said Aunt Icky.

"I did that," said Teeny.

"Then you could watch TV," Aunt Icky said.

"I already did that, too," said Teeny Witch. "And I colored pictures. I talked on the phone. I did everything there is to do in this old house."

Aunt Icky smiled. "Then you need to do something outside of this old house," she said.

Teeny Witch was puzzled.

"I know a good place to go on a rainy day," said Teeny's aunt. "It is a good place to go on any day. It is a fun place. There are lots of fun things to do there."

Teeny's face brightened. "What place are you talking about?" Teeny asked.

"I am talking about the library," said Aunt Icky.

"The library!" cried Teeny Witch. "It is not far from our house. I will go to the library."

"Have fun," called Aunt Icky as Teeny rushed out.

Teeny put on a raincoat. She put on her boots. Teeny
picked up a big umbrella and went out into the rain.
Pitter! Patter! Splatter! Pitter! Patter! Splatter!

"There's the library," Teeny shouted.

Up the library steps she scooted. "This is going to be fun," said Teeny. She walked toward the children's room. The children's room was a special place in the library just for kids. Today the children's room was having a special exhibit about pets.

Some children had brought pets to the library. The librarians had brought in pets, too. There were pets all around.

"A library is a lot more than just books," said Teeny.

Teeny looked at a goldfish in a bowl. The goldfish looked back at Teeny. Teeny smiled.

Next Teeny saw tiny hamsters. The hamsters were funny. They made Teeny laugh. She forgot all about being sad and bored. She forgot all about the rain.

There were lots of other pets on exhibit. There were birds, snakes, and even a big, hairy spider.

"Yuk!" groaned Teeny. "Aunt Vicky would like a pet like that." Teeny's Aunt Vicky had an ugly bug collection. But Teeny did not like bugs at all!

13

"It is time for the puppet show," called the librarian. "Anyone who wants to see the show, come this way."

Teeny went into a room with other children. In the room was a little puppet stage. The puppet show began.

PUPPET SHOW

15

It was a very funny show. The puppets did silly things. The children all laughed. Teeny Witch laughed the loudest of all. She liked the puppet show very much.

The librarian spoke after the show was over.
"Tomorrow is craft day in the children's room," she said.
"Tomorrow we will make baskets." The children all clapped.

"Goodness," said Teeny. "There sure are a lot of things to do in a library."

One of the best things to do in a library is to read books. Reading is lots of fun.

"I feel like reading," said Teeny. She walked over to the card catalog. The card catalog listed every book in the children's room. It told who had written each book, what it was about, and where to find the book on the shelf.

Teeny found many books that looked interesting. Some of them were fiction. That means they told stories that were make-believe. Some of the books were nonfiction. They were about real people and things that had really happened.

Teeny picked out three different books to read.
Two were fiction. One was nonfiction. She walked
over to the shelves. Each shelf had many books on it.

Teeny Witch looked for the books she wanted. She found the fiction books by looking for the name of the person who had written them. The card catalog had told her the name.

The nonfiction book had a special number that helped Teeny find it on the shelf. The card catalog had told her that, too!

Teeny took the books to a table and sat down. She opened a book. She began to read. The book was about a girl and her horse. The horse's name was Lucky. The book was very exciting.

Teeny read faster and faster. The story became more
and more exciting. Teeny pictured herself riding Lucky.

Lucky jumped over the big, white fence.

Lucky jumped very high.

Go Lucky go!

"Faster, Lucky! Go faster," Teeny called. Lucky jumped over a big fence. "Wheee," said Teeny.

"Did you say something?" a boy at Teeny's table asked.

"No," replied Teeny. "I was just excited. This book is very good."

The boy smiled at Teeny. "I know," he said. "I read that horse book yesterday."

Teeny finished her book and started a new one.

The next book was about space. It had lots of pictures in it. In the book people rode in spaceships. People had robots to help them.

"The future looks exciting," thought Teeny Witch. She thought about the future. She thought about spaceships and robots.

Teeny Witch pictured herself in the future. She saw herself riding in a spaceship.

She saw herself with a robot helper. The robot was helping her clean her room. The robot was picking up her toys.

"Having a robot would be fun," thought Teeny Witch.

Teeny Witch put down the book. There wasn't time to read the next book. It was time to go home.

"I will take this last book home with me," said Teeny.

Teeny put two books back. She took the other book to
the librarian. Teeny gave the librarian her library card.
A library card lets you take books home. The card is
easy to get.

The librarian smiled at Teeny Witch. She checked out
Teeny's book. "You have to bring this book back in two
weeks," said the librarian.

"I will," promised Teeny.

"I had fun today," said Teeny.
"Good," said the librarian. "Come back tomorrow.
We will have fun again."

"I think I will come back tomorrow," said Teeny.
"Goodbye," said the librarian.

Teeny put on her raincoat. She put on her boots.
She put her book under her raincoat to keep it dry.
Teeny always took good care of library books.

With her umbrella in her hand Teeny went out. But she did not need her umbrella. It had stopped raining. The sky was bright.

When Teeny got home she found two of her aunts on the porch.

"Hi, Aunt Ticky," called Teeny. "Hi, Aunt Vicky."

"Hi," said Aunt Ticky. "What did you do on this awful day?"

"Today was great," replied Teeny. "I had lots of fun."

Aunt Ticky looked at Aunt Vicky. They were puzzled. "Where did you go? What did you do?" asked Aunt Vicky.

Teeny Witch smiled. "I saw a pet exhibit," said Teeny. "I saw a puppet show. I picked out three books all by myself. I rode on a horse named Lucky. Lucky and I even jumped over a fence."

"You jumped over a fence?" asked Aunt Vicky.
Teeny nodded. "Then I flew in a spaceship. I even had
a robot help me pick up my toys."

Aunt Vicky looked at Aunt Ticky. Now she was more puzzled than ever.

"Where did Teeny go today?" asked Aunt Vicky.

"I don't know," said Aunt Ticky. "I thought she just went to the library."

"I did," laughed Teeny Witch. And she went inside to read her new library book.